Presented to
BGSU University Libraries
Curriculum Resource Center
The Frances F. Povsic Collection

Donated by:

The Publisher &
Cooperative Services for
Children's Literature

WHERE IS WOODSTOCK?

BY CHARLES M. SCHULZ

Spotlight

visit us at www.abdopublishing.com

Reinforced library bound edition published in 2013 by Spotlight, a division of the ABDO Group, PO Box 398166, Minneapolis, MN 55439. Spotlight produces high-quality reinforced library bound editions for schools and libraries. Published by agreement with Peanuts Worldwide, LLC.

Printed in the United States of America, North Mankato, Minnesota.
102012
012013

 This book contains at least 10% recycled materials.

Library of Congress Cataloging-in-Publication Data

This book was previously cataloged with the following information:

Schulz, Charles M. (Charles Monroe), 1922-2000.
Where is Woodstock? / by Charles M. Schulz.
p. cm. -- (Peanuts Picture Books)
[1. Birds--Juvenile fiction. 2. Dogs--Juvenile fiction. 3. Camping--Juvenile fiction.
4. Scouts and scouting--Juvenile fiction. 4. Nature--Juvenile fiction.]
PZ7.S38877 Wi 2008
[E]

2008298918

ISBN 978-1-61479-033-4 (reinforced library edition)

All Spotlight books are reinforced library bindings
and manufactured in the United States of America.

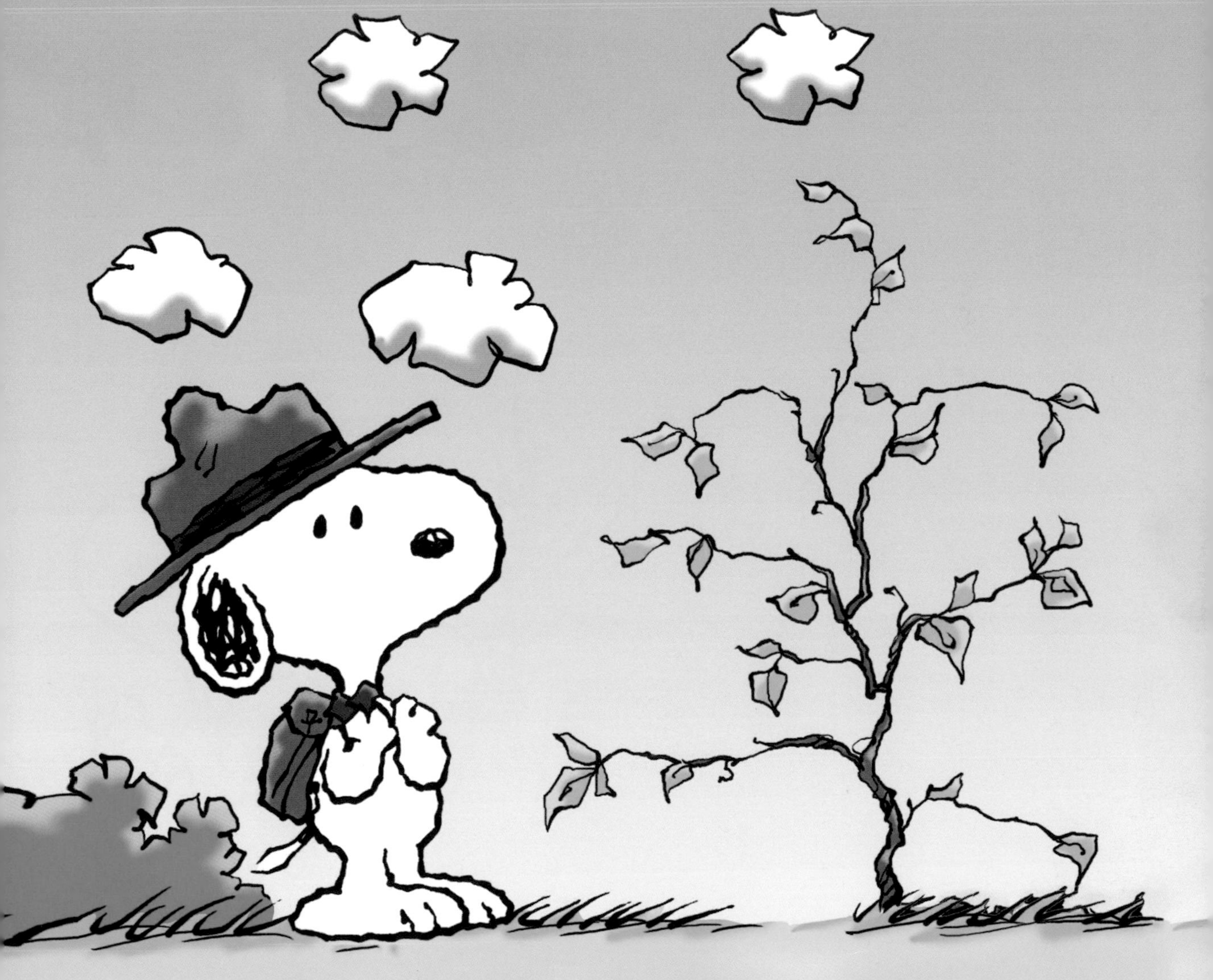

Alright scouts, before we go on our hike
I am going to call the roll!

Conrad! Oliver! Bill! Harriet! Woodstock!

Now that everyone is here,
let's start our hike!

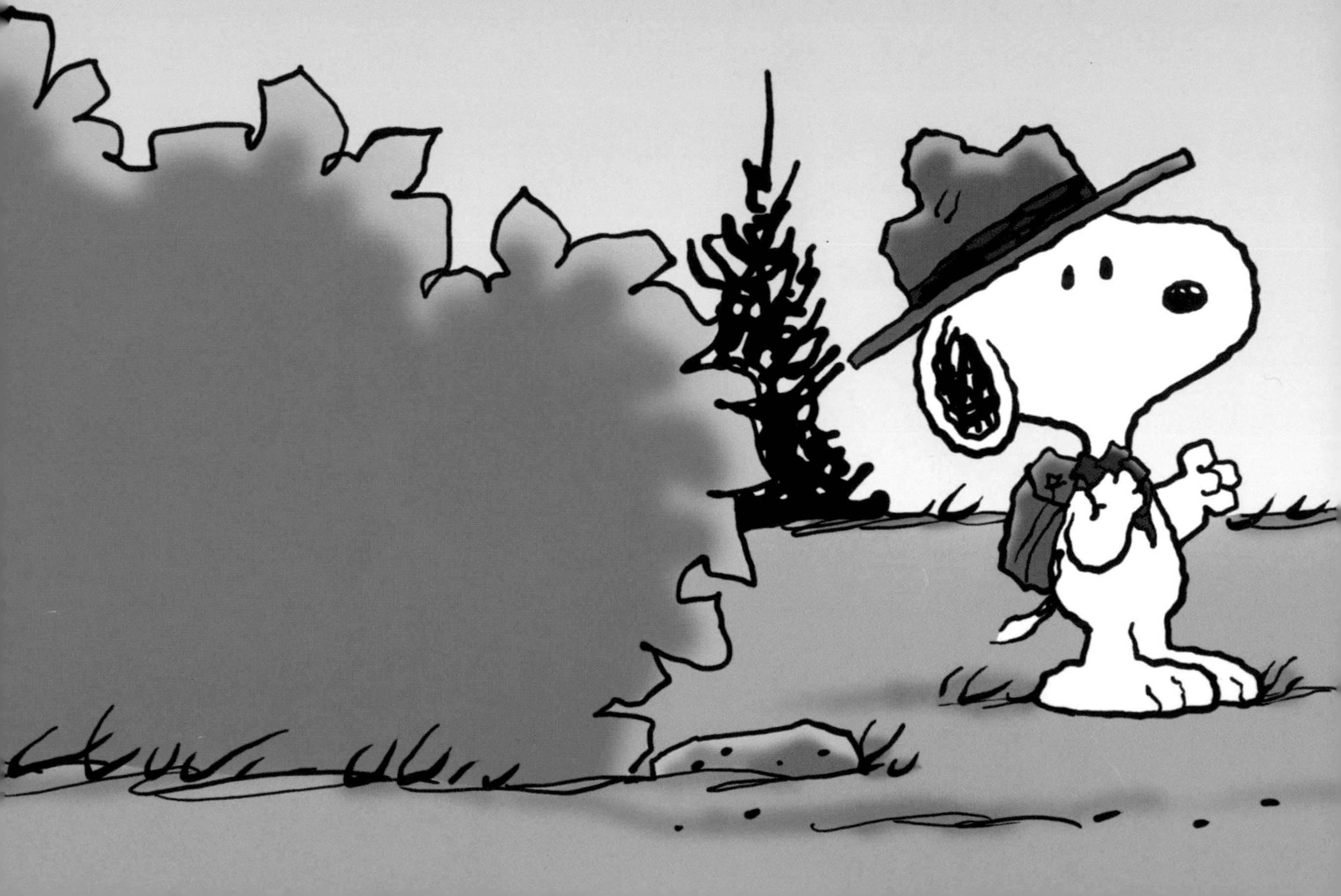

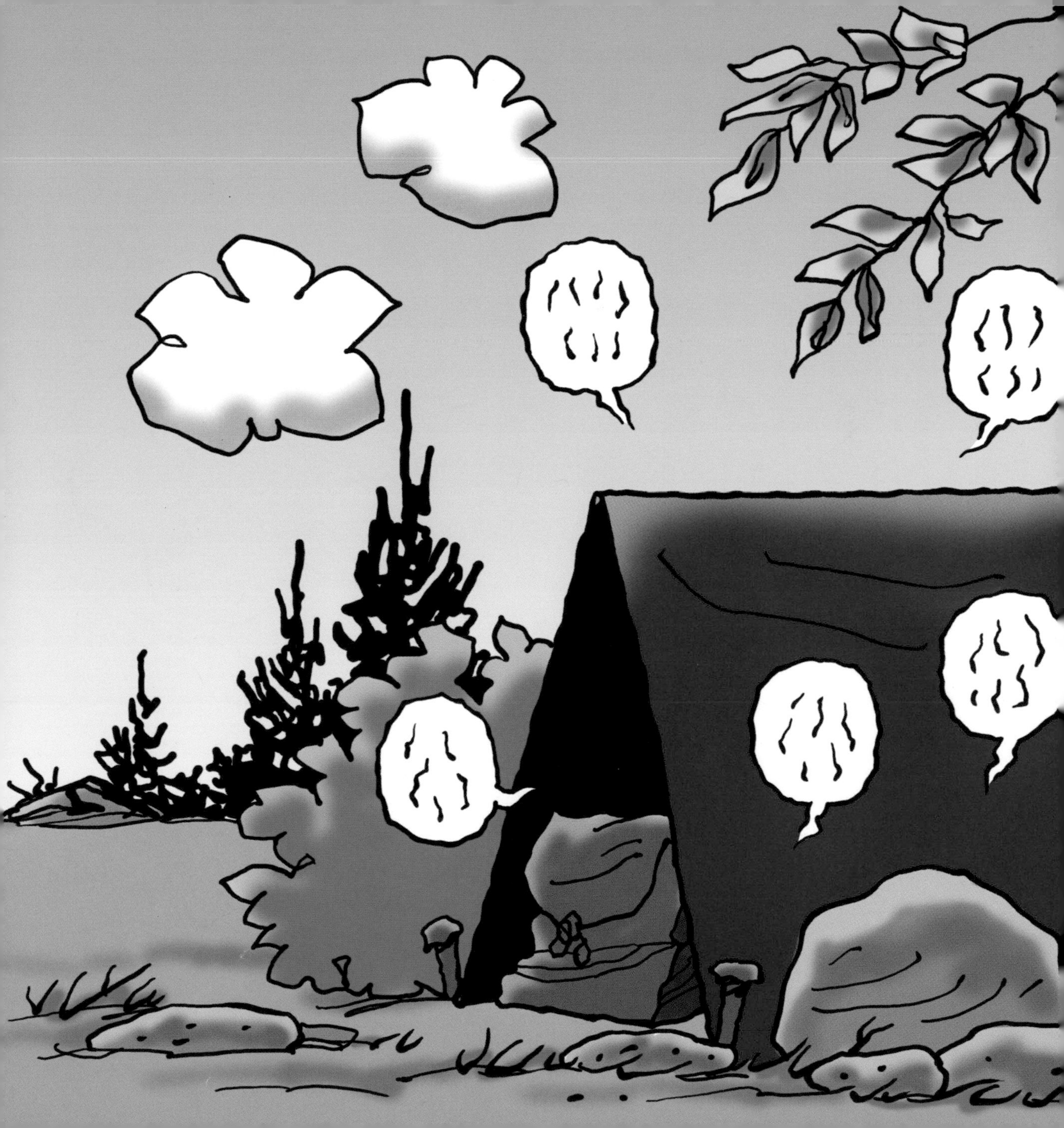

OK troops, today I'm going to give you a lesson in survival.
Let's say we are lost in the woods . . .
what would we do about food?

Shoot a moose?
Good answer Bill but no . . .

Speaking of lost . . . where is Woodstock?

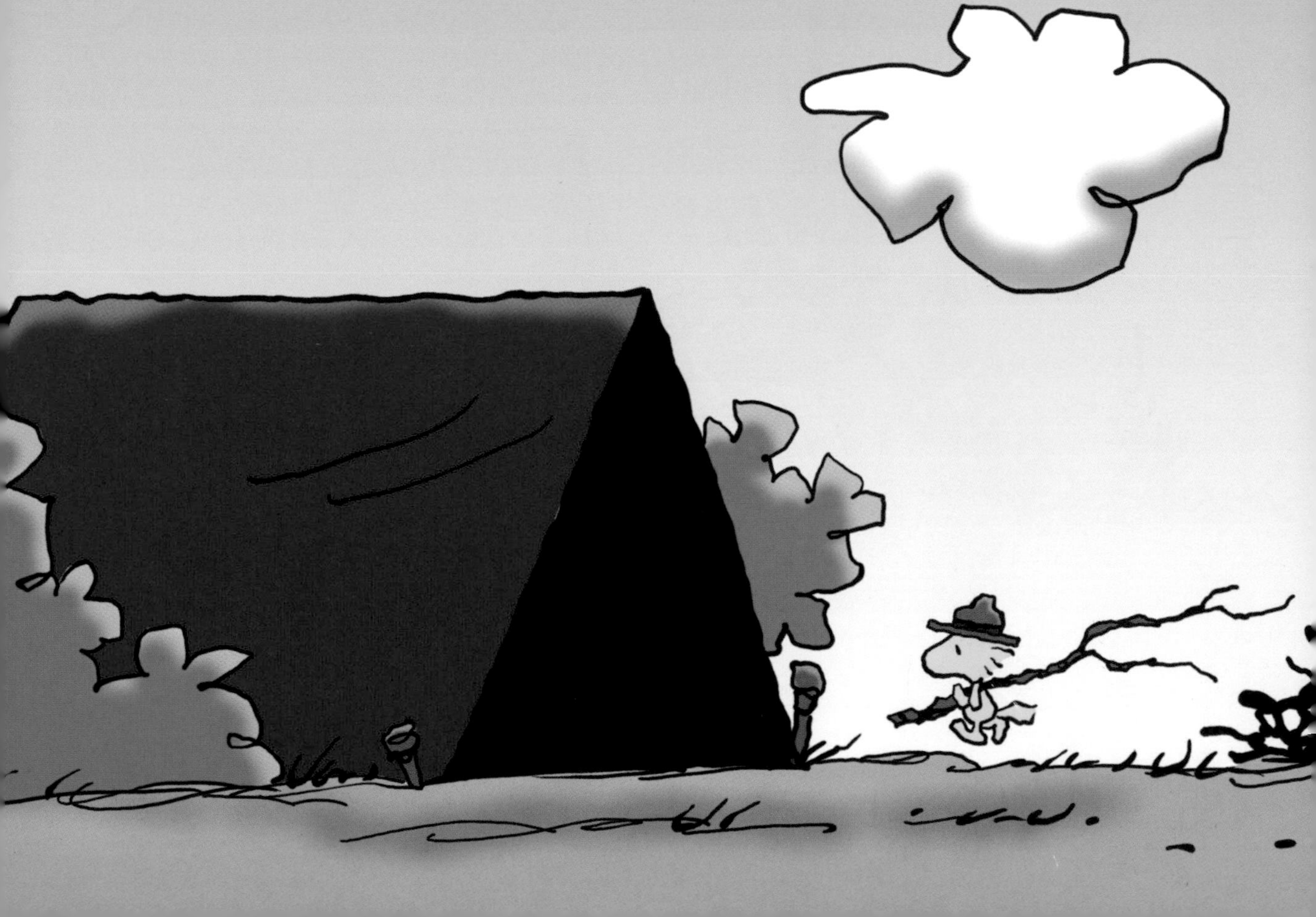

Conrad—fly off and find
Woodstock.

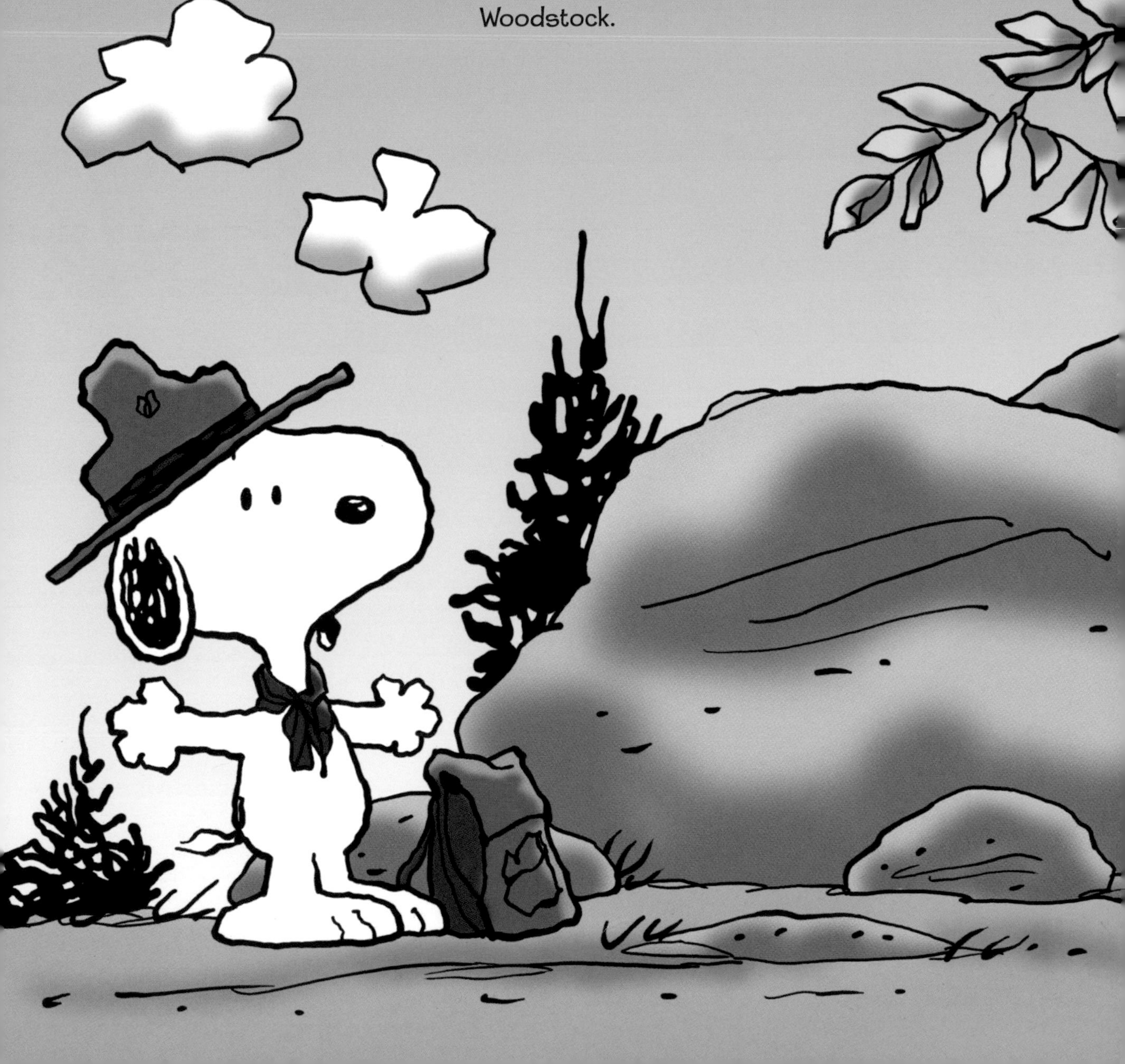

If I were lost in the woods, you know what I would do? I'd open this can of tennis balls. You know why I'd open this can of tennis balls? Because when I was packing my gear I thought it was a tall can of soup.

Where are Woodstock and Conrad?

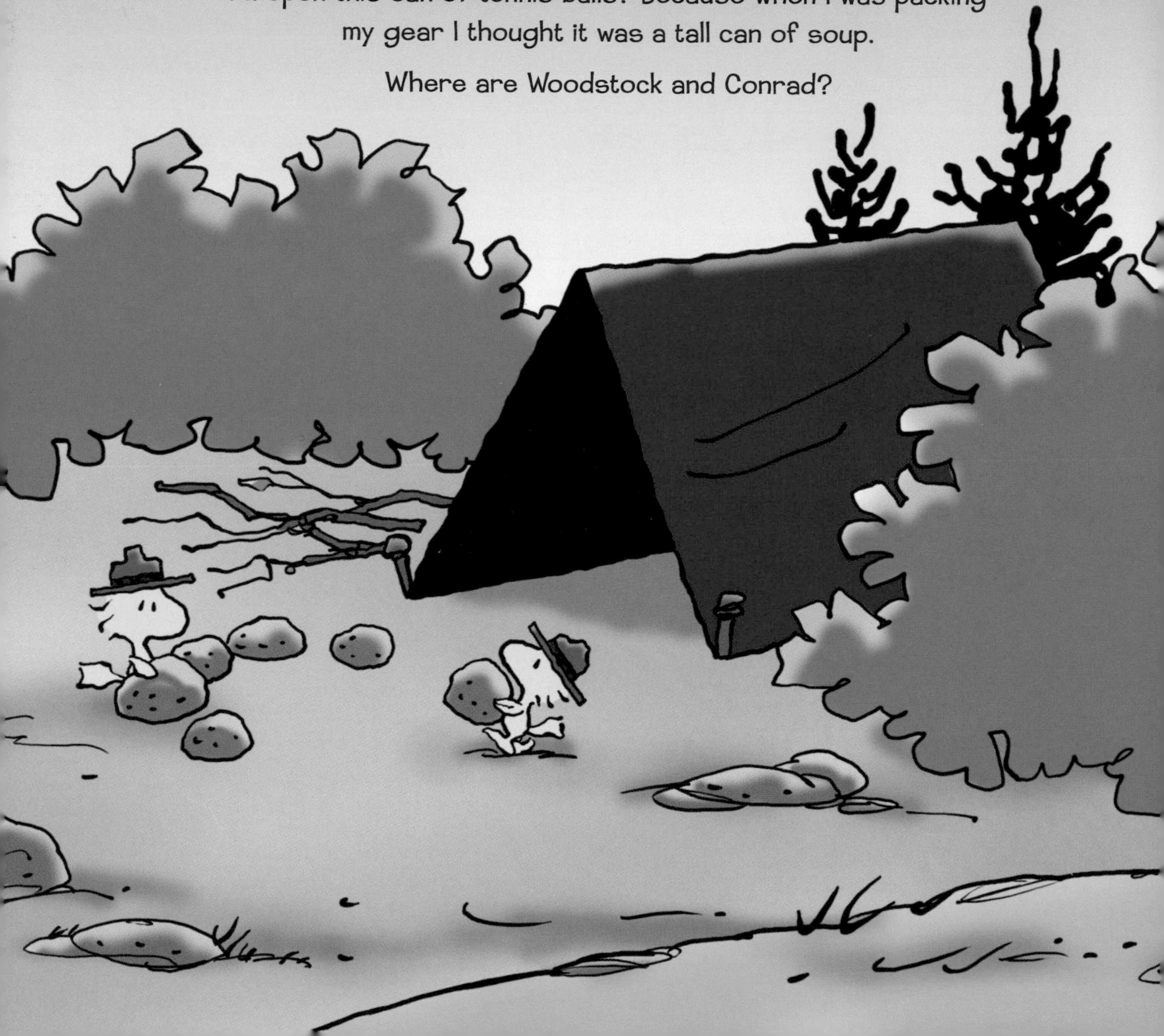

Harriet—fly off and
find Woodstock and Conrad.

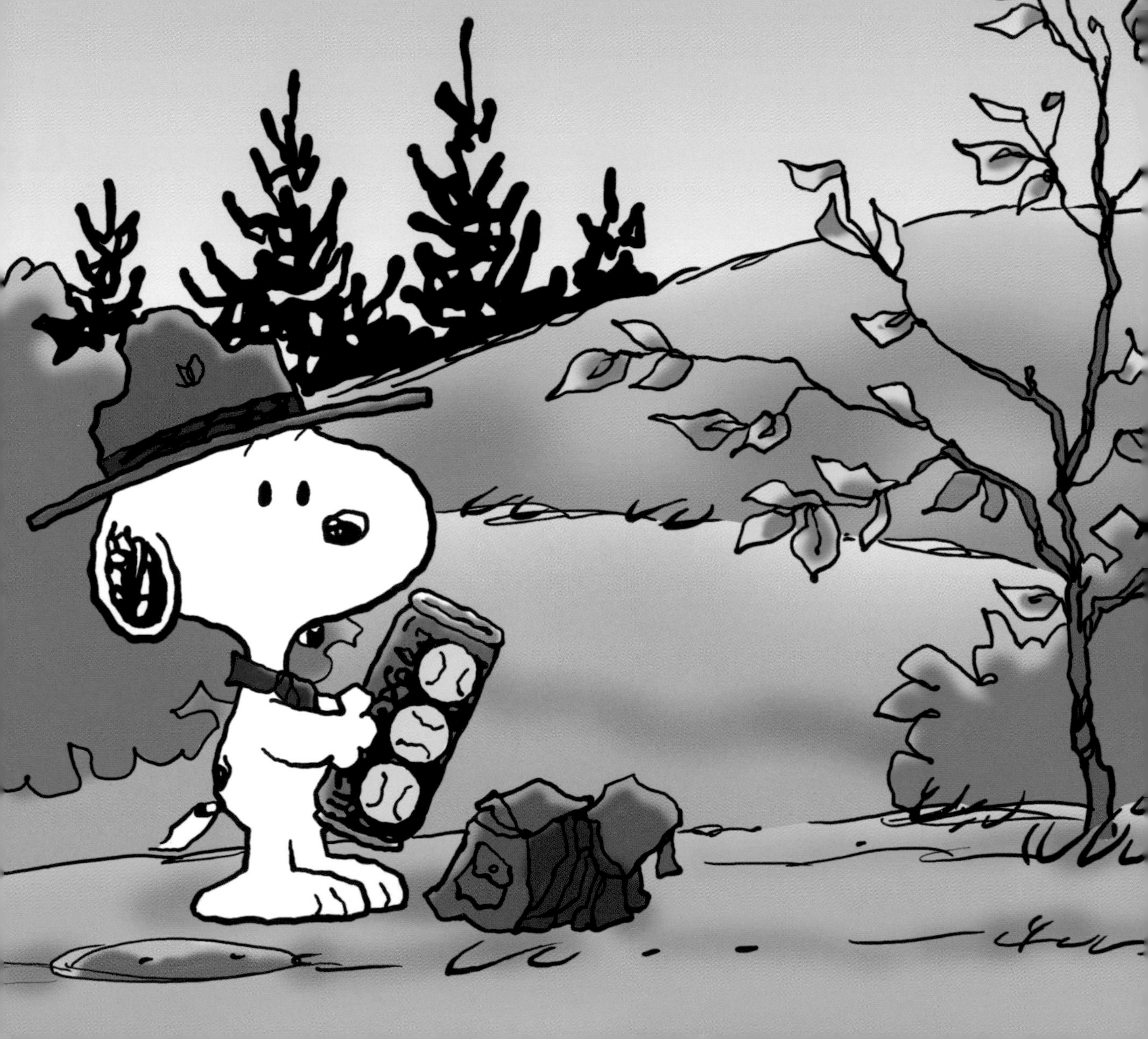

The wilderness is inhabited by many different creatures.
Some are friendly and some are dangerous.
What is the best way to protect ourselves from snakes?
Sitting on top of my hat is one option.

I wonder what happened to Woodstock, Conrad, and Harriet?

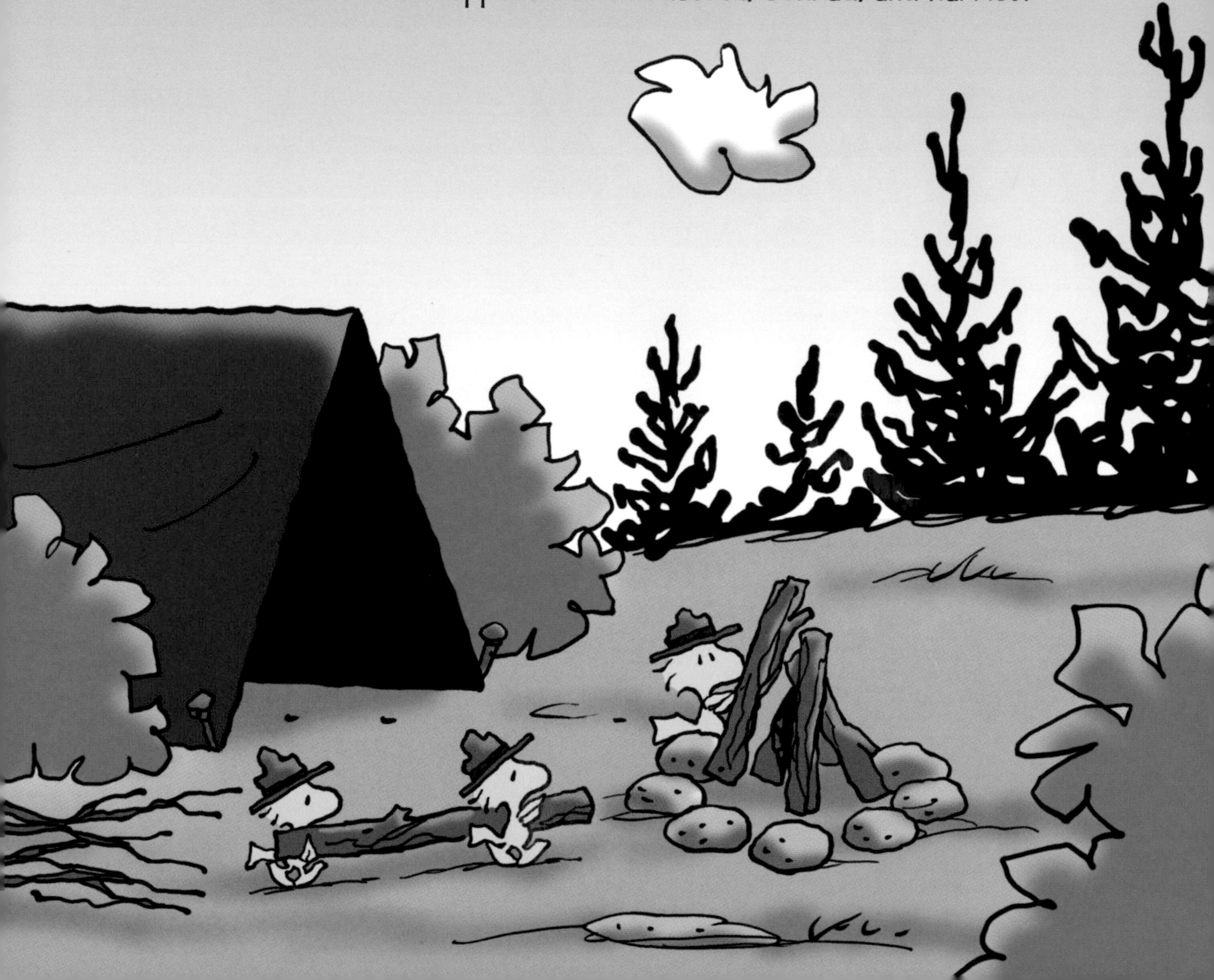

Bill—fly off and find
Woodstock, Conrad, and Harriet.

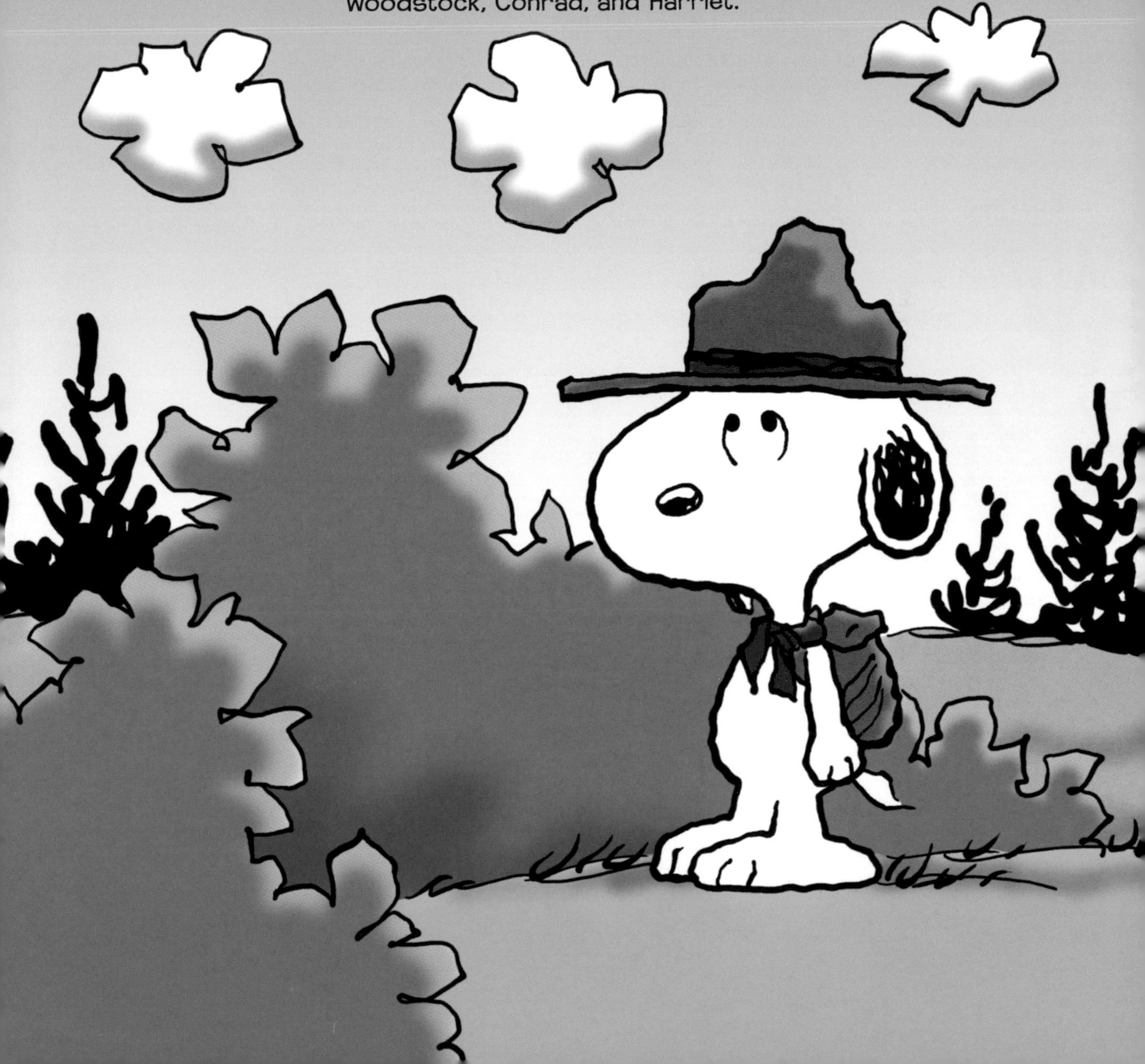

Well, Oliver . . . It looks like we lost our Beagle Scout troop.
What are we to do?

You suggest going back to camp? You are right!
Maybe we will find Woodstock, Conrad, Harriet, and Bill there.

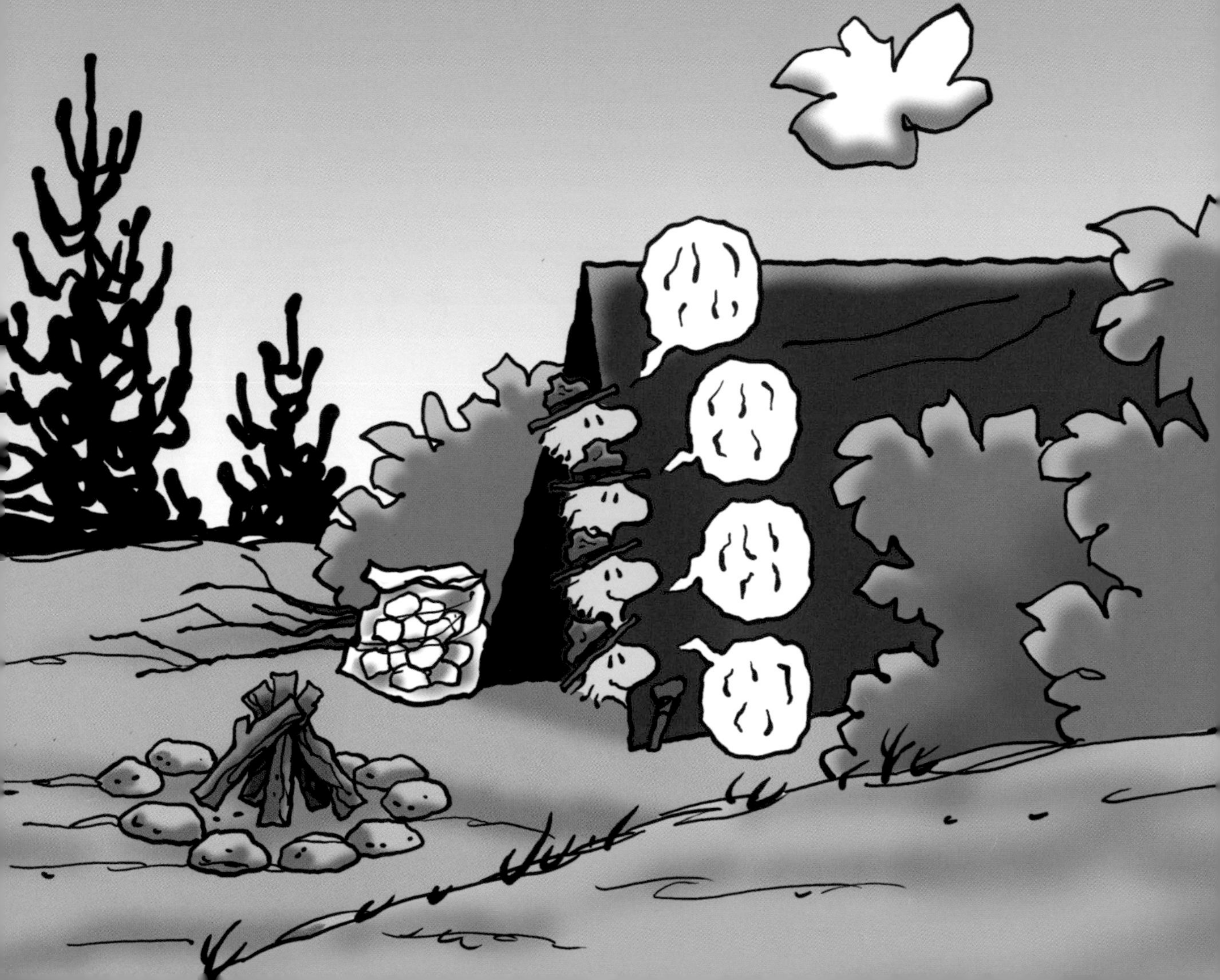

Oliver—you lead the way!

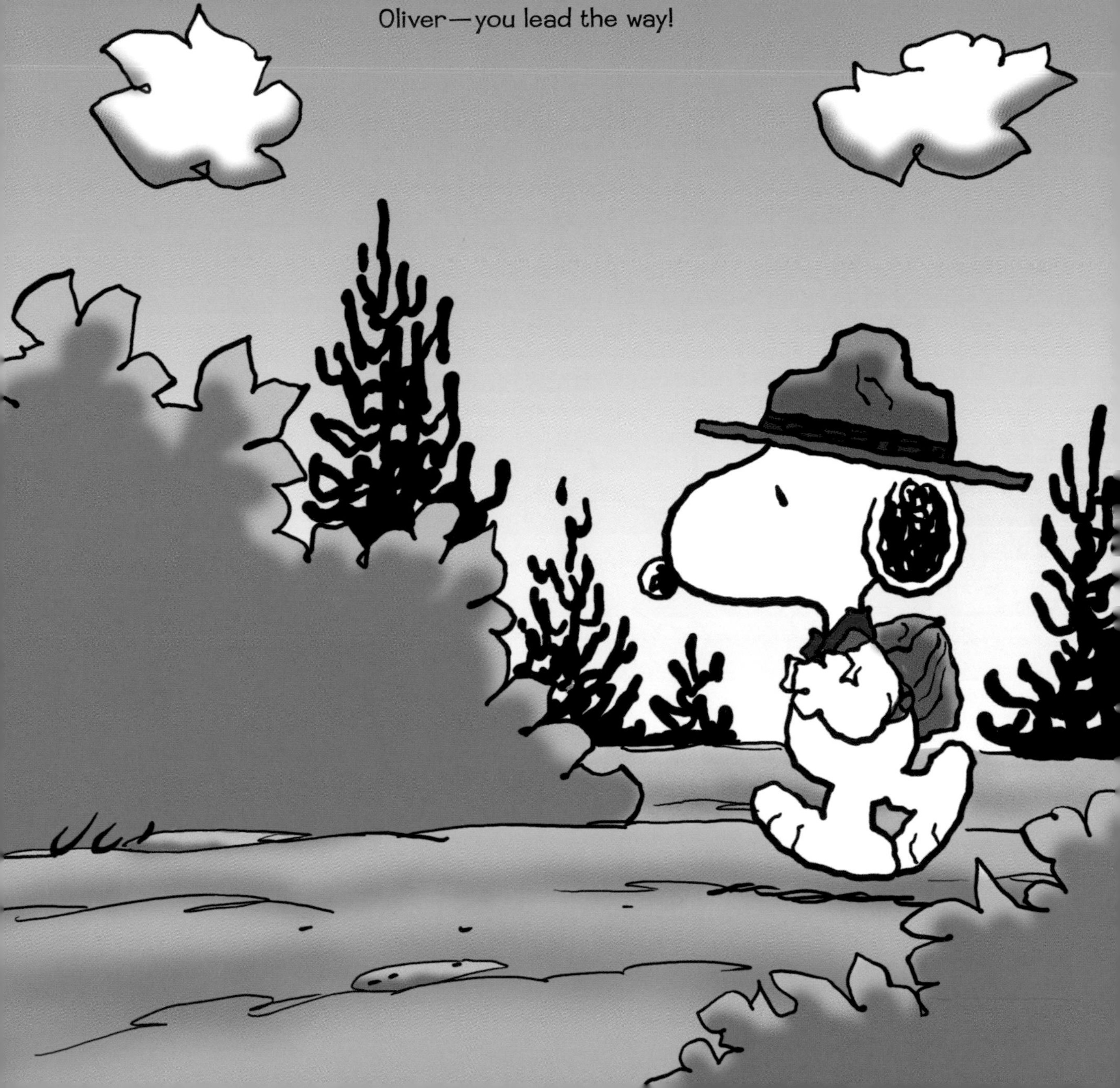

I was wondering where my troops disappeared to.
Am I surprised? Of course! For our last night of scouting
I think a marshmallow roast is a great idea!

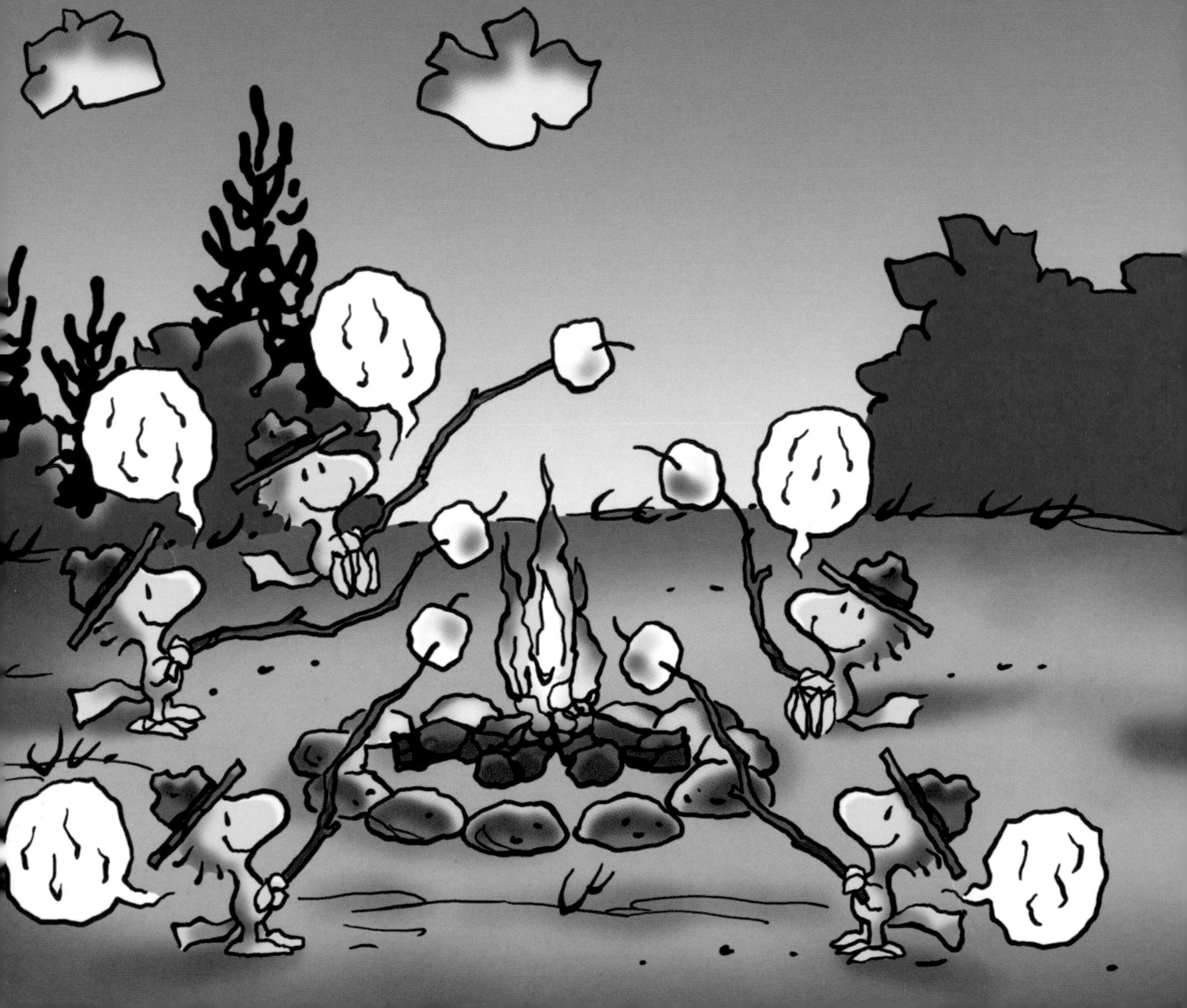

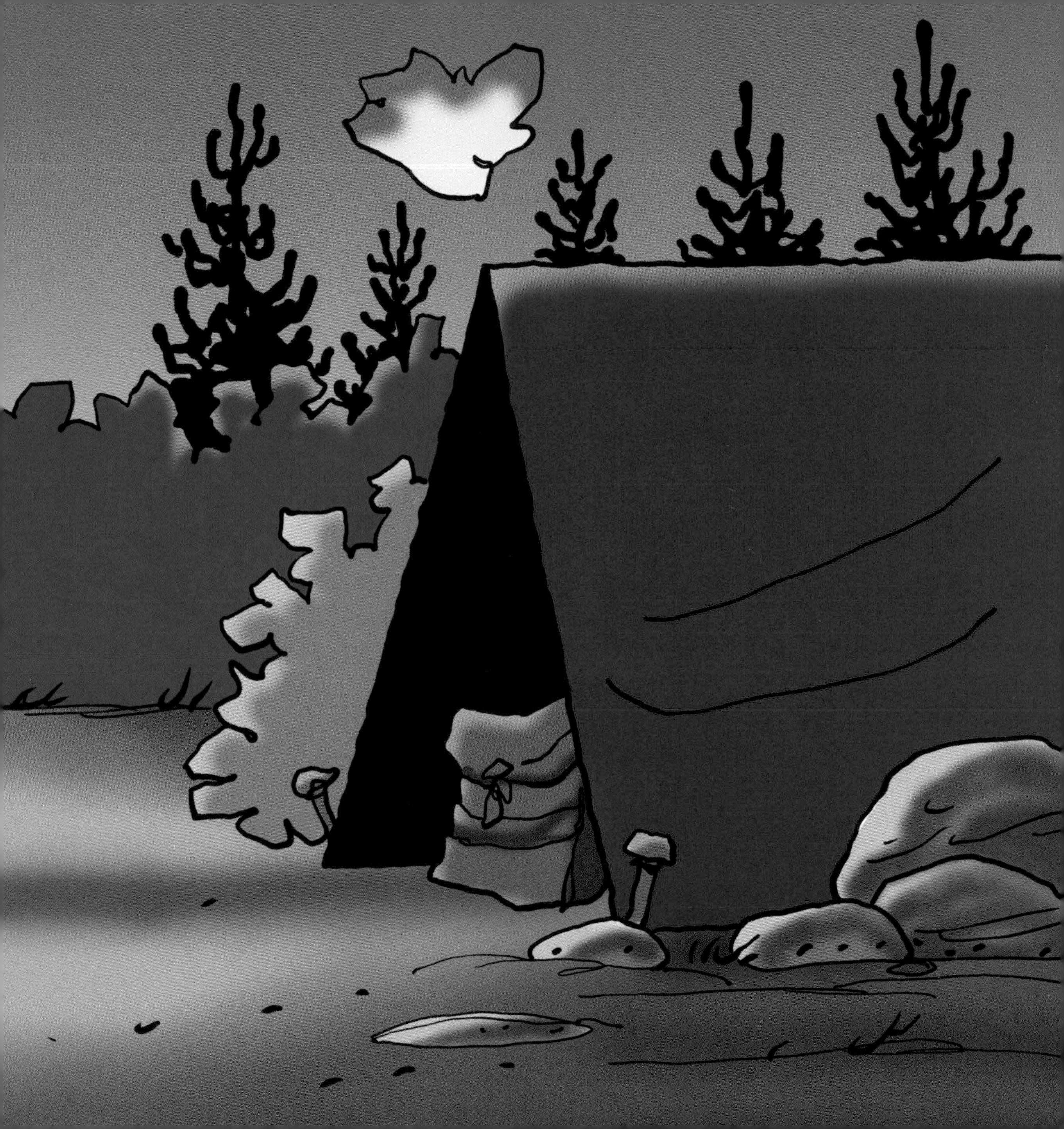

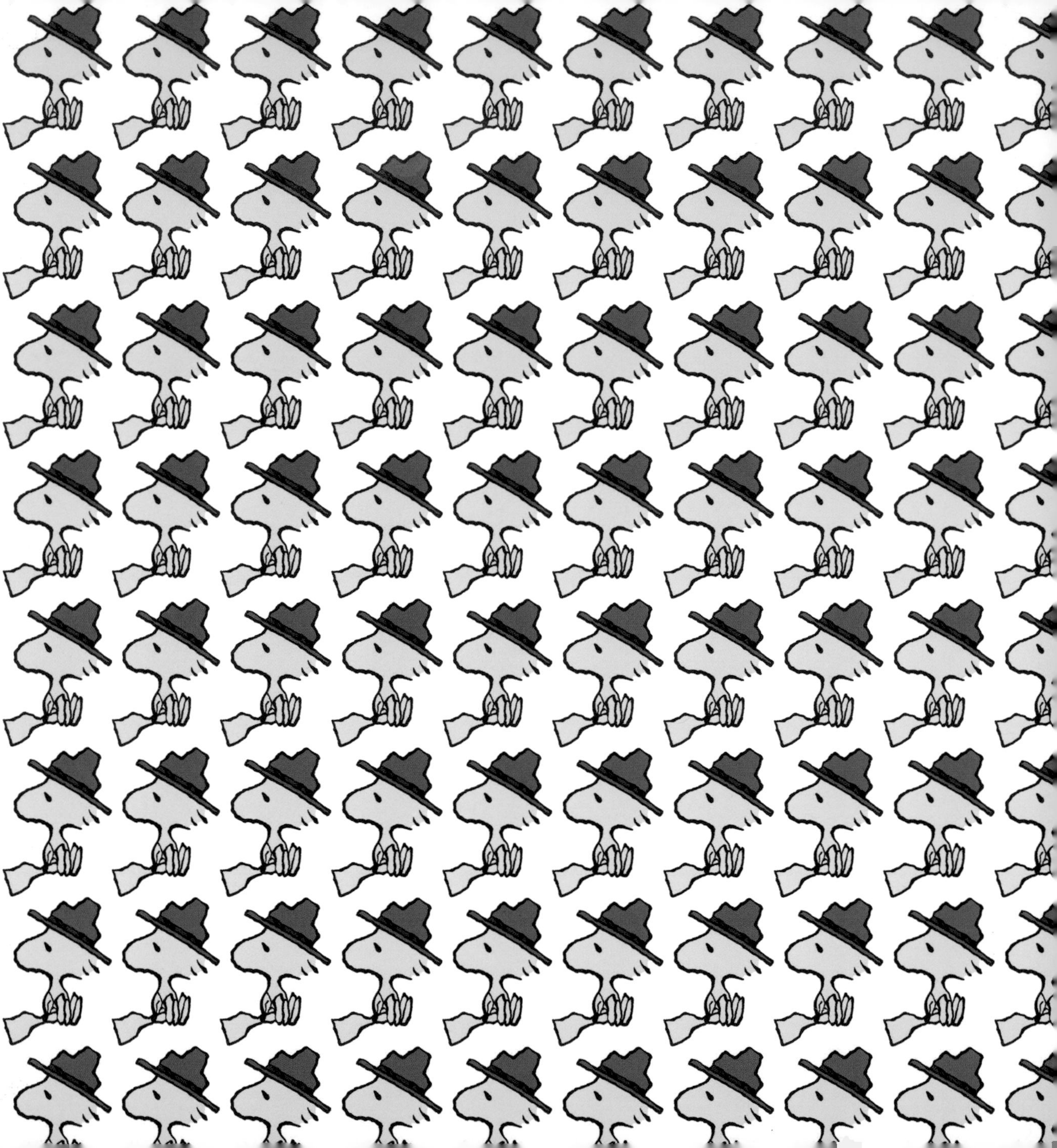

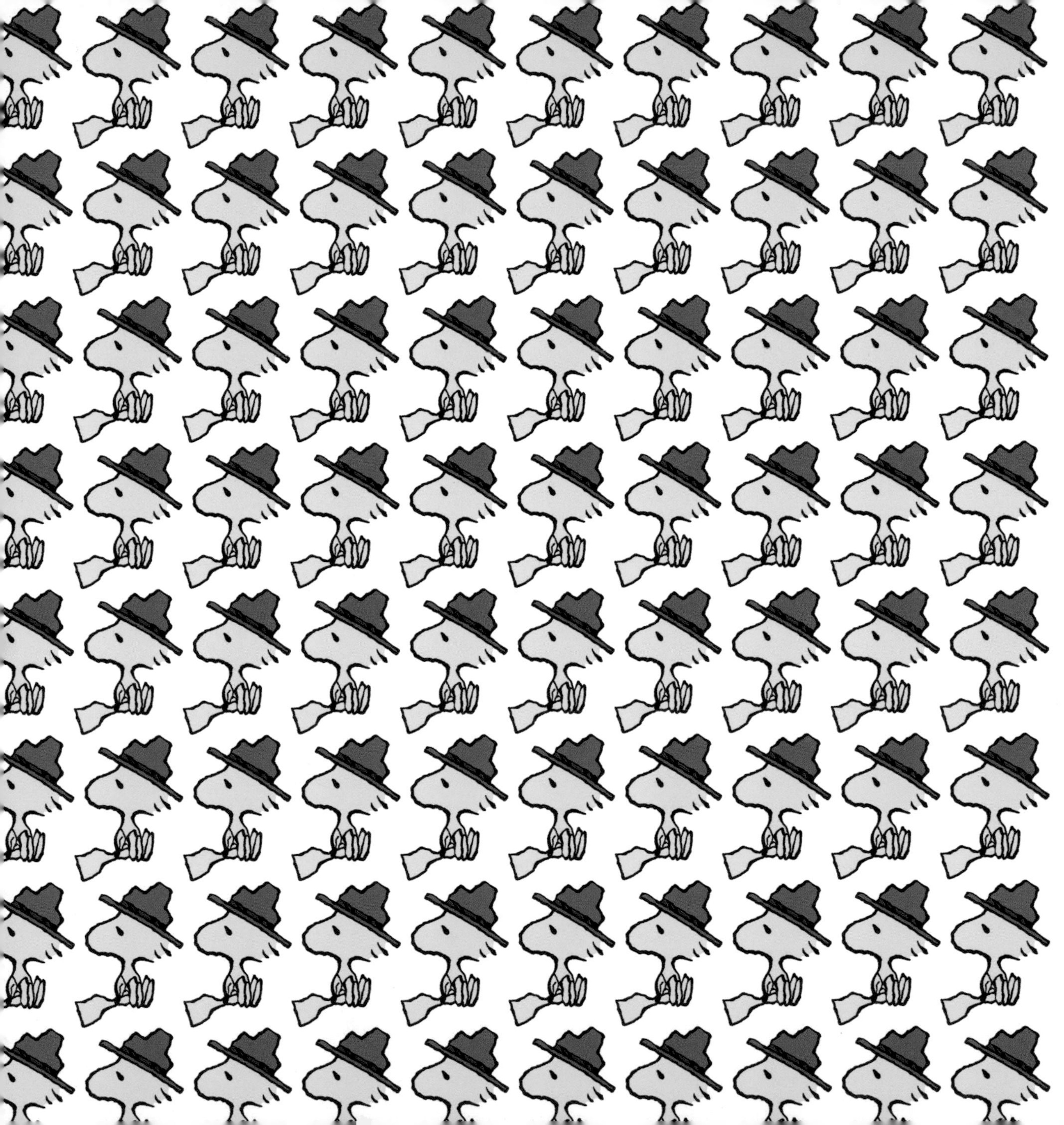

DATE DUE

APR 1 0 2014		
JUN 7 2013		
MAY 1 8 2014		
JUL 1 5 2014		
JUL 2 1 2014		

GAYLORD

PRINTED IN U.S.A.